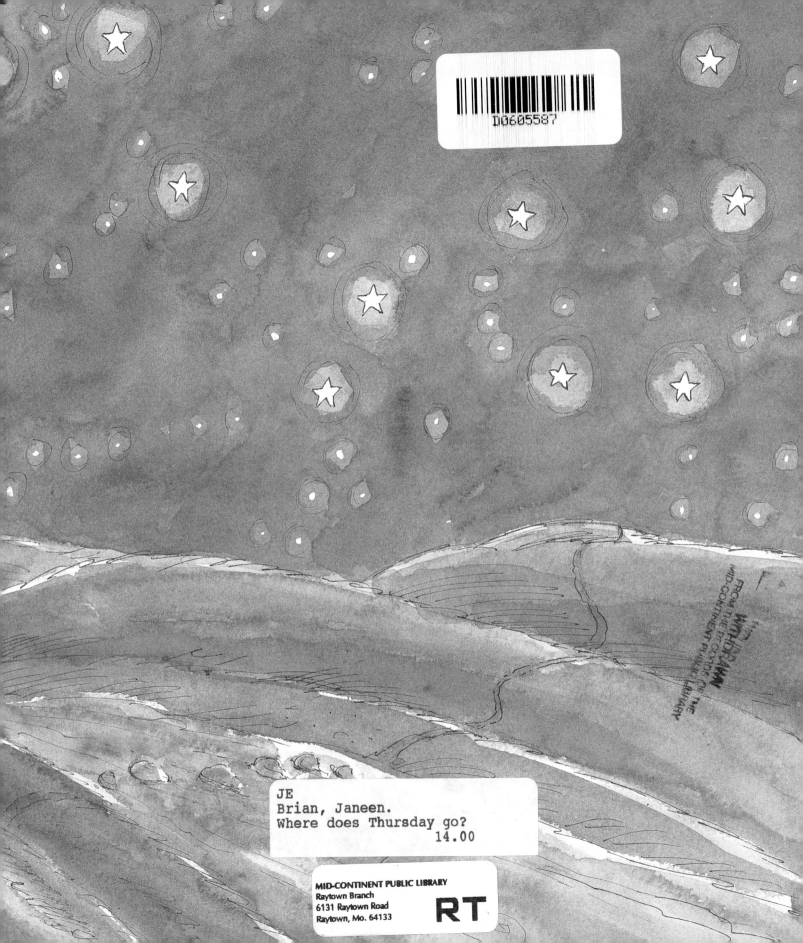

Where
does
Thursday
go?

Love to Liam Christopher, for his birthday. JB

For Jane, Niev, and Mr Finn. SMK

Clarion Books
a Houghton Mifflin Company imprint
215 Park Avenue South, New York, NY 10003
Text copyright © 2001 by Janeen Brian
Illustrations copyright © 2001 by Stephen Michael King

First published in Australia in 2001 by Margaret Hamilton Books,
an imprint of Scholastic Australia Pty Ltd,
PO Box 579, Gosford NSW 2250.

The text was set in 20-point Garamond Classic.
The illustrations were executed in ink and watercolor.

For information about permission to reproduce selections from this book,
write to Permissions, Houghton Mifflin Company,
215 Park Avenue South, New York, NY 10003.

www.houghtonmifflinbooks.com

Printed in Singapore.

Library of Congress Cataloging-in-Publication Data

Brian, Janeen
Where does Thursday go? / words, Janeen Brian ;
pictures, Stephen Michael King.
p. cm.
Summary: Bruno and Bert try to find out what happens to a
special day after it is over.
ISBN 0-618-21264-7
[1. Days—Fiction. 2. Bears—Fiction. 3. Birds—Fiction.]
I. King, Stephen Michael, ill. II. Title.

PZ7.B7587 Wh 2002   [E]—dc21   2001047187

10 9 8 7 6 5 4 3 2 1

Where does Thursday go?

Words
Janeen Brian

Pictures
Stephen Michael King

Clarion Books • New York

It was Thursday.

Bruno's birthday.

What fun they all had!

That night, Bruno thought about
his special day and wished it didn't have to end.
He knew his birthday would be gone
in the morning.

So, wondered Bruno, what happened
to it during the night?

Where did it go?

"**Where** does Thursday go before Friday comes?" he asked his friend, Bert.

Bert looked thoughtful.
"It has to go somewhere," said Bruno.

"I'd like to say goodbye to it before it goes.
Come on."

They crept downstairs and slipped
out into the star-speckled streets.

First they came to a bridge.
A gentle river gurgled beneath.

"Oogle, gurgle. Oogle gurgle," it said.

"Is that you, Thursday?" Bruno called out.
"We've come to say goodbye."

But there was no reply.

Bruno and Bert found a park.
"Toowhit! Toowhoo!"
called an owl from a tall tree.

As it flapped past, its wings whispered
in the cool night air.

"Is that you, Thursday?" called Bruno.
But there was no reply.

Bruno and Bert sat down by the edge of a lake.
A streak of shining silver swam past with a flick of its tail.

"Is that you, Thursday?" called Bruno.
But there was no reply.

The friends climbed a hill.
Suddenly, a deep growl whooshed out of a tunnel.
"Whoo! Whoo!" cried the engine, and
its wheels hummed as it raced past.

"Is that you, Thursday?" called Bruno.
But there was no reply.

BRUNO and Bert walked to the edge
of the sea. White-tipped waves splashed the shore.

"Swish, Swish," the waves sighed as they
drew back into the ocean.

"Is that you, Thursday?" called Bruno.
But again, there was no reply.

Sadly,
Bruno
and
Bert
turned
toward
home.

They sat down on the front steps.
"Do you know what I think Thursday looks like?" said Bruno.
Bert looked interested.

"I think it's big and round,
                like my birthday cake,"
                said Bruno.

"And it's bright, like my candles,

and it makes me happy, like balloons," said Bruno.
"I think Thursday is all of these things."

Bert looked very thoughtful.

And he glanced up at the sky.

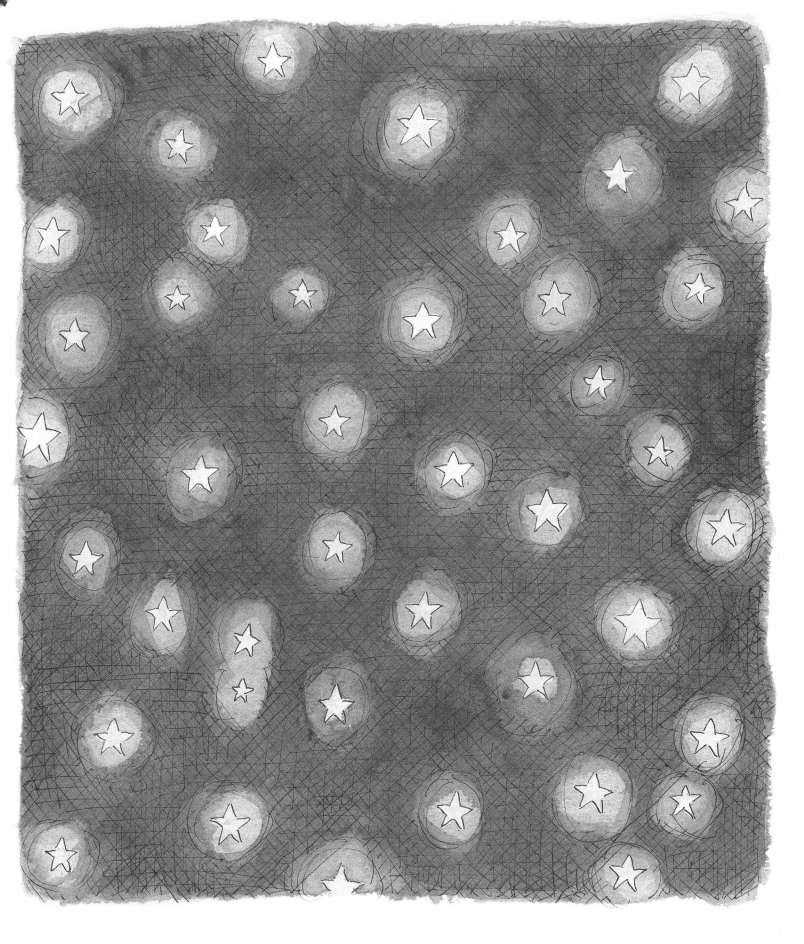

There was the moon,
big and round and bright,

hanging like a silver balloon.

Just like . . .

Thursday!

Just then, the moon began to drift slowly behind a cloud.
Bruno waved.

"Goodbye, Thursday!"

he called.

"Goodbye."

Then Bruno and Bert
crept back inside.

They climbed into bed,

closed their eyes,

and slept soundly until . . .

the sun brought Friday.

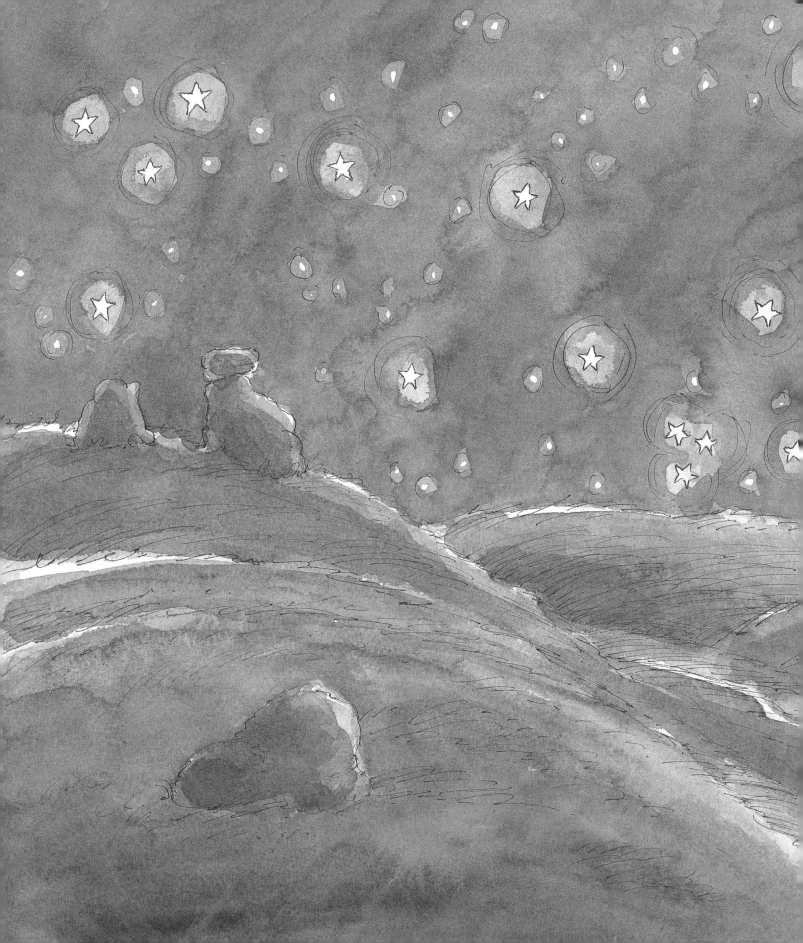

PRESENTED TO

. . . .

FOCUS ON THE

CELEBRATE

Gary Smalley and

FAMILY PRESENTS
THE FAMILY

John Trent, Ph.D.

TYNDALE HOUSE PUBLISHERS, INC. WHEATON, ILLINOIS

Visit Tyndale's exciting Web site at
www.tyndale.com

Designed by Timothy R. Botts

Library of Congress Cataloging-in-Publication Data

Smalley, Gary.
  Celebrate the family / Gary Smalley and John Trent.
  p. cm.
  ISBN 0-8423-1055-X (hc : alk. paper)
  1. Family Pictorial works. 2. Family–United States
Pictorial works. 3. Christians Portraits. 4. Christians–
United States Portraits. 5. Family–Religious aspects–
Christianity. I. Trent, John T. II. Title.
HQ525.C5S6 1999
306.85'022'2–dc21   99-26398

Printed in United States of America

08 07 06 05 04 03 02 01 00 99
10 9   8   7   6   5   4   3   2   1

Contents

CONTENTS

*I*t is no secret that the family is under attack in nearly every country of the world. What is not as widely known is that the family is surviving and even thriving in the face of unprecedented challenges from governments and general moral decline. What is it about the family that makes it so resilient? Many believe that the family is instituted by God and survives because of His grace and mercy.

Dr. James C. Dobson, founder and president of Focus on the Family and author of many books that have blessed and encouraged millions of families, gives us this insight into the nature and importance of families:

The eternal plan for the family, as I understand it, begins with a lifelong commitment between a man and a woman, undergirded by absolute loyalty and fidelity to one another. The husband then devotes himself to the best interests of his wife, providing for her needs and protecting her to the point of death if necessary. The wife honors her husband, devotes herself to him, and respects his leadership in the family. If they are blessed with children, those children are recognized to have inestimable worth and dignity–not for what they produce or accomplish, but for who they are as God's own handiwork.

INTRODUCTION

The children are taught while very young to yield to the authority of their parents. Boundaries of behavior are established in advance and then enforced with reasonable firmness. They learn honesty, integrity, humility, self-control, personal responsibility, sexual purity, concern for others, the work ethic, and the fundamentals of their faith. They are never subjected to humiliation, rejection, sexual exploitation, or abuse of any kind. Instead, they enjoy unconditional love and are raised "in the fear and admonition of the Lord."

Let me leave you with this thought: When you and I have reached the end of our brief journey on this earth, nothing will matter more to us than the quality of our families and the depth of our relationship with God. "Meaning" in this human experience is drawn essentially from these two sources. If that is true, then should we not live by those priorities every day that remains to us?

As you read the word pictures that Gary Smalley and John Trent have written alongside the beautiful photographs of families, try to imagine the stories of the families you are meeting and discover the connections between these families and your own. Although

they come from all over the world and represent a variety of cultures and circumstances, the differences will not seem as significant as the similarities. The love, growth, and joy that are unique to family life shine through no matter where we live or what situations we face.

We hope that your heart will be warmed by the joy on the faces of these moms, dads, children, grandparents, and friends of families and that your spirit will be encouraged as you sense the love that binds these families—and yours—together. Our prayer is that as your family members experience this book together, you will be challenged to recommit yourselves to one another so that your family will enjoy the full blessings the Lord has for you. It's time to celebrate the family.

The Publisher

FOR THIS REASON A MAN WILL LEAVE HIS
FATHER AND MOTHER AND BE UNITED TO
HIS WIFE, AND THE TWO WILL BECOME ONE
FLESH. THIS IS A PROFOUND MYSTERY–BUT I
AM TALKING ABOUT CHRIST AND THE
CHURCH. HOWEVER, EACH ONE OF YOU
ALSO MUST LOVE HIS WIFE AS HE LOVES
HIMSELF, AND THE WIFE MUST RESPECT HER
HUSBAND.

E P H E S I A N S   5 : 3 1 - 3 3

ONE
MARRIAGE
Two Becoming One

The Begin of

It begins with that spark of attraction that develops into keen attention. Men and women find one another in as many ways as there are couples. The beginning of romance is full of excitement, anticipation, anxiety, and hope. Every movement or phrase is full of meaning no one else can comprehend. The pace at which two people learn about each other is incredible. This first phase of love is so exhilarating that no one could keep up such intensity forever. ◆ Then the real relationship begins. The excitement gives way to a season of exploration–thinking, talking, learning one another's history and personality, loves and fears. As time goes by, romantic flush becomes honest care. Finally two people make a daring commitment–to love one another in mind, body, and soul for the rest of their lives. ◆ Love's journey into marriage is unlike other ventures. In God's care it transforms the worlds of both people and all other people they touch. The biblical bond of marriage uplifts and strengthens both partners, giving them a fertile environment in which to develop as people–and grow in God's love and grace.

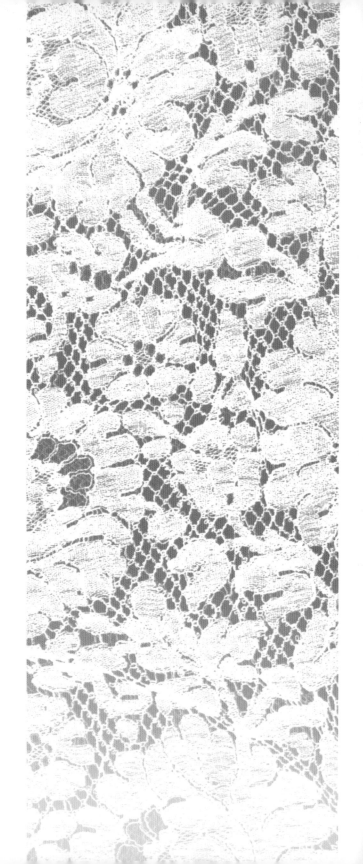

precious
My husband treats me like a priceless antique. He walks in, picks me up, and holds me with great care and tenderness. I often feel as if I'm the most precious thing in our home. He saves the best hours and his best efforts for me.

gentle

When I awoke this morning, I got to thinking about how your love is like a snowflake. It is gentle, soft, and unique in every way. Like an evening snowfall, your love blankets me when I awaken.

Two are better than one because they have a good return for their labor. For if either of them falls, the one will lift up his companion. . . . And if one can overpower him who is alone, two can resist him.

ECCLESIASTES 4:9-12 (NASB)

7

trans

planted

I felt like an acorn that had been tossed into a pile of rocks. I never had the right amount of light or the proper soil, so I grew into an oak tree that was bent and crooked. But in the few years since we've been married, I feel that you have done the impossible. You've transplanted me to a place in the sun, where I can at last grow straight and tall.

direction

Our marriage is a lot like a raft trip. There are times when I take us down an uncharted section of the river, and we overturn and everything gets soaked. But I never see you complain. I know I tend to go off on a new idea without looking at a map, but you never hold it against me. I know I'm blessed to have you.

*M*any, O Lord
my God, are the
wonders you have done.
The things you planned
for us no one can
recount to you; were I to
speak and tell of them,
they would be too
many to declare.

P S A L M   4 0 : 5

11

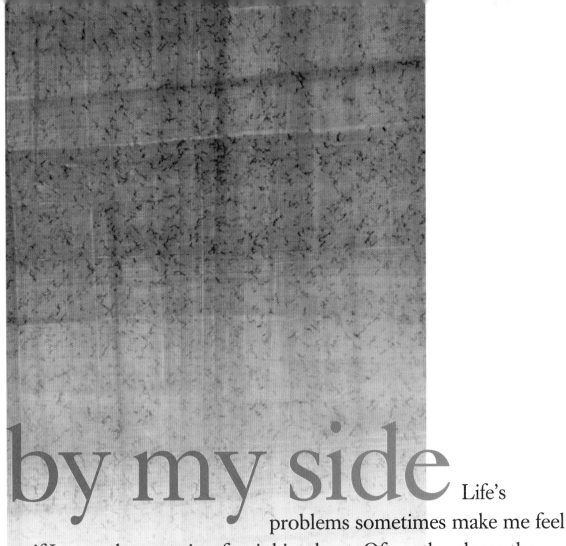

by my side

Life's problems sometimes make me feel as if I were the captain of a sinking boat. Often, the closer the boat gets to going under, the more those around me dive overboard and leave me to save the vessel by myself. I'm thankful to have a "first mate" who stays by my side no matter what. If it weren't for her and the strength and help she gives so freely and lovingly, I would have given up and jumped overboard a long time ago.

HER CHILDREN ARISE AND CALL HER
BLESSED; HER HUSBAND ALSO, AND HE
PRAISES HER: "MANY WOMEN DO NOBLE
THINGS, BUT YOU SURPASS THEM ALL."

P R O V E R B S   3 1 : 2 8 - 2 9

TWO
MOTHERS
*Nurturing Body
and Soul*

Your

in This

She is your first source of everything–food, warmth, affection, safety. As you grow into a little person, her heart follows your every step and misstep. Like Mary, the mother of Jesus, she is continually storing up in her heart all that you do, all that you learn, and all that she learns about you. ◆ Her comfort and care are unique in a world of varied relationships. She knows you better than you usually want to admit. She roots for you when your goals seem impossible, and she picks up the pieces when plans come apart.

◆ Mother–whatever her age, her traits, her struggles, or her circumstances–is your anchor in this world. She is where your world began, and there will always be a certain strength and wisdom that comes only from her.

on top

of the world

When I see my children and how well they're doing in life, pride swells within me like snowcapped mountains above a green valley. It's a feeling like I'm on top of the world. My children have moved away now, and most of the time the mountains stand at quite a distance. Yet even from afar, looking at them fills me with wonder and thankfulness.

potential
In some ways you're like the bud of a flower–full of potential but so fragile. Sometimes I get frustrated when you don't open up and share your feelings with me. But I've learned that if I'm patient and wait until you're ready, you'll bloom and share with me in a beautiful way.

*W*e were gentle
among you, like a
mother caring for her
little children. We loved
you so much that we
were delighted to share
with you not only the
gospel of God but our
lives as well, because
you had become
so dear to us.

1 THESSALONIANS 2:7-8

thankful
Because of my children's constant affirmation, I feel like a beautiful, well-groomed show horse. My coat shines, and my beautiful mane dances as I parade about. I often go out for a run with other show horses, and many of them feel abused and misused by their children. I'm so thankful for the kids I've got and the way they reflect love.

*T*hen they rose early in the morning and worshiped before the Lord, and returned and came to their house at Ramah. And Elkanah knew Hannah his wife, and the Lord remembered her. So it came to pass in the process of time that Hannah conceived and bore a son, and called his name Samuel, saying, "Because I have asked for him from the Lord."

1 SAMUEL 1:19-20 (NKJV)

sparkle
You are a beautiful and delicate gift from God. Looking at you is like looking at a work of art, skillfully crafted by masters. Every part of you is unique and perfect in its own way. You sparkle in a rainbow of light, and every day as I watch you grow, I catch a new reflection of why I love you so much.

sweet

My mom's love is like a huge ice-cream sundae! It is sweet and fun, and no matter how much I want, there's always more than enough to go around, not only to me, but to all my brothers and sisters as well.

HOW GREAT IS THE LOVE THE FATHER HAS LAVISHED ON US, THAT WE SHOULD BE CALLED CHILDREN OF GOD! AND THAT IS WHAT WE ARE! 1 J O H N 3 : 1

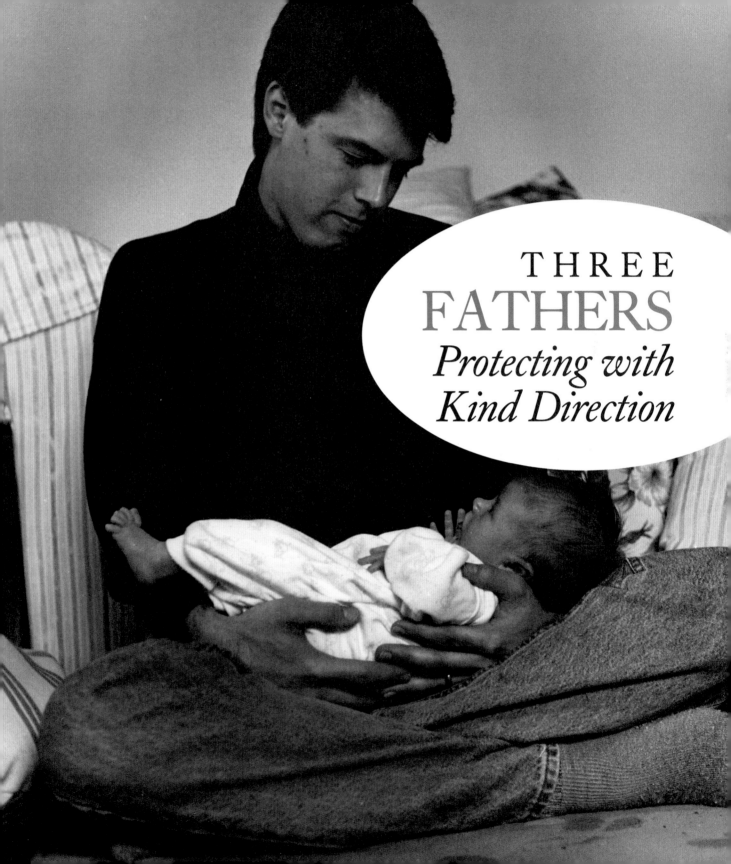

THREE
FATHERS
Protecting with
Kind Direction

In His Strong

30

Our need for Daddy exists before we even understand it. As infants, we have no way of knowing who he is or what he gives us. We don't understand that his love and support of Mommy enables her to love and support us. His face and voice may not be the first face and voice we bond to. But once we discover him and know what it is to be held in his strong grasp, we understand safety and love in a whole new way. ◆ A father's love and acceptance supply security we find nowhere else. Daughters need to know they are beautiful and worthy of respect. Sons need to know that they can overcome problems and find strength even in weakness. When Daddy has confidence in us, no other opinion counts. ◆ A father may be young, vibrant, and successful. Or he may be up in years, dealing with illness or other setbacks. But in his children's eyes, a loving father's strength never falters.

doughnuts

I feel like the guy on the doughnut commercial. With working and taking care of three kids, it's always "time to make the doughnuts." But there's still nothing as sweet as doing just what I'm doing.

provider

I feel like a nesting hawk. Using every sense I have, I gather food for my young ones and watch carefully for any predators who might be after them. Tiring at times? Sure. Yet I've never felt more important and useful. I cherish the demands of guarding and loving my children.

You know
how we exhorted,
and comforted, and
charged every one of you,
as a father does
his own children,
that you would walk
worthy of God
who calls you into
His own kingdom
and glory.

1 THESSALONIANS 2:11-12

(NKJV)

35

36

rewards
When I've survived a long day's work, the trip home can feel like a walk through the desert with no end in sight. But after struggling through the heat, the trail does end, and there's this brilliant pool of cool water. At last I'm at a place where I can drink and be refreshed. That's what it's like being with my children.

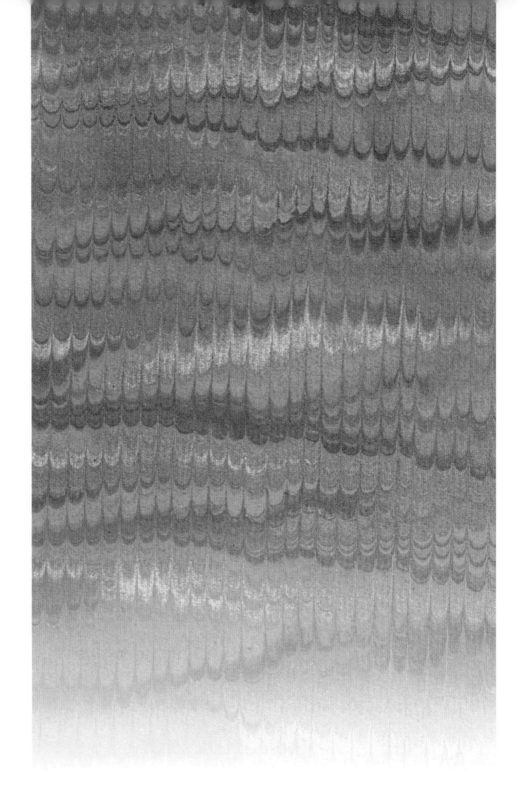

38

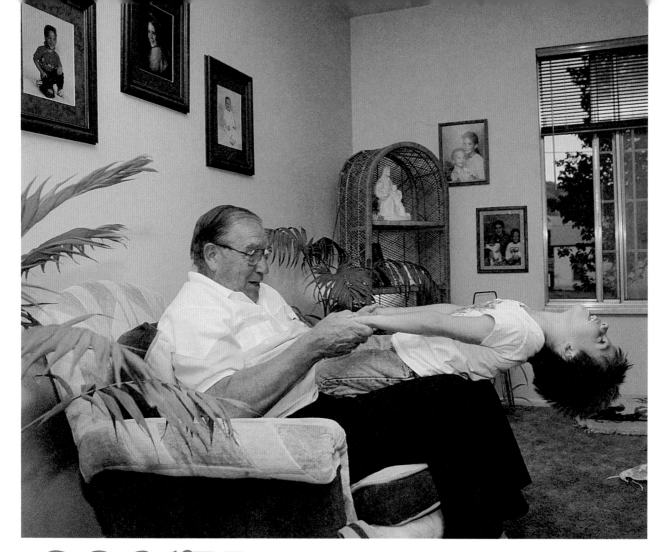

scary

For years my dad was too busy to spend any time with us kids or his grandchildren. But God has given us a miracle, and all of that has changed. Whenever I see Dad holding my son, it's a bit like being at the beginning of a huge amusement-park ride. It's a little scary, but it's so exciting, and I hope the ride never ends.

returning

home

Returning home from a business trip is like taking a quiet drive in the country after driving a taxi in New York City for a week. No one is cutting me off or yelling at me. There are no red lights to frustrate me or crummy drivers to swerve into my path. When I come home to my kids, I'm on the street where people actually wave because they like me and are glad to see me.

THEN OUR SONS IN THEIR YOUTH WILL BE
LIKE WELL-NURTURED PLANTS, AND OUR
DAUGHTERS WILL BE LIKE PILLARS CARVED
TO ADORN A PALACE. P S A L M   1 4 4 : 2 1

FOUR
CHILDREN
Growing from One Miracle to the Next

Dangers
Possibi

When children enter our lives, the world becomes a different place. It is full of dangers and possibilities that we have never faced before. Children give us new eyes and ears—we can explore and enjoy the world around us all over again. ◆ When we experience a child's development, we come face-to-face with the grace of God. Will my daughter recover from this illness? Will my little boy keep up in school? Will they make good choices and grow to love God and other people? We love and guide as much as we can. But ultimately these little people who came from us make their own decisions, and we must learn to trust God to watch over them. ◆ As we feel our love well up for our children, we understand better how God's love wells up for us. As we watch our daughters and sons make their way in the world, we understand how God longs for us to stay in touch with Him and ask for help when we need it. ◆ A child is one of God's most awesome gifts to us. The love we pour out for that child is just one more gift we give back to our heavenly Father.

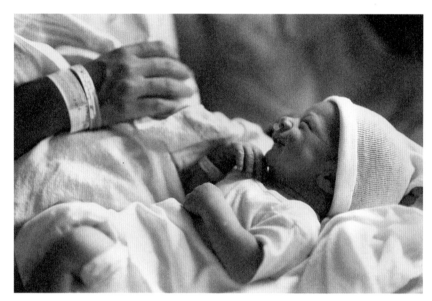

too
won

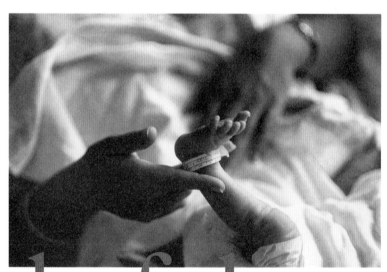

derful When I watched my daughter being born, it was as if God had led me to a sandy beach and was showing me an ocean full of future blessings that my daughter would bring. It's all been too wonderful to comprehend, too beautiful to believe.

shine

My grandchildren are like stars in a desert sky. Each has a brilliance all its own and a unique place in creation. Like those stars, my grandchildren glimmer in their own special way. They burn brightly with love for others. I hope that for as long as they live they will shine with the love I see now.

*C*hildren's children
are a crown to the aged,
and parents are the
pride of their children.

P R O V E R B S   1 7 : 6

remember

ing

When my children go out of their way to call and come by, I feel that I've been surprised with a gift. You expect a present at Christmas. But nearly every week I get a card, a call, or a visit from one of my children. I get Christmas presents all year long!

dance
I was born with a physical disability, and when people express doubts about my ability to do something, I feel like a bumblebee. They look at me and say, "Aerodynamically, there's no way you can fly!" But my parents look at me and say, "The way you were made, you can't help but fly!" I've been buzzing around ever since!

*J*esus said, "Let the
children alone, and do
not hinder them from
coming to Me;
for the kingdom
of heaven belongs
to such as these."

MATTHEW 19:14

(NASB)

rising

The love that I have for my children is so solid and enduring–like a mountain rising out of the plains. They can always look to it, receive comfort from its presence, and know that it will always be there.

WHO SHALL SEPARATE US FROM THE LOVE OF CHRIST? SHALL TROUBLE OR HARDSHIP OR PERSECUTION OR FAMINE OR NAKEDNESS OR DANGER OR SWORD? . . . FOR I AM CONVINCED THAT NEITHER DEATH NOR LIFE, NEITHER ANGELS NOR DEMONS, NEITHER THE PRESENT NOR THE FUTURE, NOR ANY POWERS, NEITHER HEIGHT NOR DEPTH, NOR ANYTHING ELSE IN ALL CREATION, WILL BE ABLE TO SEPARATE US FROM THE LOVE OF GOD THAT IS IN CHRIST JESUS OUR LORD. R O M A N S 8 : 3 5 - 3 9

FIVE
TOUGH TIMES
*When Families
Grow Together*

A New

of

A family learns a lot about itself during less-than-perfect times. Along with emotional ups and downs, ruined plans, and chronic inconveniences come opportunities for children to discover Mom and Dad's true priorities. When life gets difficult, Mom and Dad have the opportunity to model patience, resourcefulness, and faith. ◆ When we look back on the tough times, we can see God's hand even in what seemed to be chaos. We can remember the unexpected laugh that found us in the middle of a desperate situation. We may feel relief that we got through it and gratefulness that things still turned out all right. We might also know a new level of faith, since we've weathered so much already.

◆ Tough times teach parents to trust God—to see their children through to the other side, to help Mom and Dad do the right thing under stress. These times teach children that there is help beyond Mom and Dad and that godly love is the source of strength and peace.

genuine

I have a special friend who has an amazing ability to help me overcome my faults. She's like a skilled surgeon, with a keen eye for diagnoses and a sharp mind to wisely discern how best to solve the problem. When it's time for surgery, she soothes the pain with an anesthetic of genuine love and concern. Then when the surgery is over, she gently closes the wound with tender stitches of compassion. But what I like about her the most is that, like any good surgeon, she constantly checks up on my progress and assures me I'll be better because of the operation.

For me, life is sometimes like waterskiing. The towline is unexpectedly jerked, and I fall headlong. I try it again, only to be dumped once more and left in the water, shivering, exhausted, and alone. Just when I'm ready to give up, my wife lovingly speeds to my rescue. In an instant she throws out a lifeline, and I pull myself from the water's icy grip. With her I am warm, safe, and loved. My wonderful wife has rescued me again!

life

*Do not be
anxious about anything,
but in everything,
by prayer and petition,
with thanksgiving,
present your requests
to God.
And the peace of God,
which transcends
all understanding,
will guard your hearts
and your minds in
Christ Jesus.*

PHILIPPIANS 4:6-7

line

63

storms

There have been times over the years when I've faced hailstorms that I thought would turn into tornadoes. But I've always been able to run to my father, who's been a protection from hardship. He's like a storm cellar, and I know that he'll be there when the dangerous weather blows into my life.

Those who trust in the Lord are like Mount Zion, which cannot be shaken but endures forever. As the mountains surround Jerusalem, so the Lord surrounds his people both now and forevermore.

PSALM 125:1-2

*W*ho can find a
virtuous wife? For her
worth is far above
rubies. The heart of her
husband safely trusts her;
so he will have no
lack of gain. She does him
good and not evil
all the days of her life.

PROVERBS 31:10-12 (NKJV)

on the

inside

Before I lost my leg in an accident, I felt like any other apple in a barrel. But for a long time after my surgery, I felt like I was rotten inside and out and totally worthless to anybody else. Yet my wife has never viewed me any differently. She knows I don't look like everyone else on the outside, but on the inside I've never changed. To her I am unique and complete.

after all

these years
I feel a lot like an old sewing machine. I've been faithfully running for years, but I'm not as fast as I used to be. I squeak more often these days. That's why it's such a blessing to have friends who give me the oil of encouragement and support. With them I know I have many years of faithful service left!

THROUGH WISDOM A HOUSE IS BUILT, AND
BY UNDERSTANDING IT IS ESTABLISHED; BY
KNOWLEDGE THE ROOMS ARE FILLED WITH
ALL PRECIOUS AND PLEASANT RICHES.

P R O V E R B S   2 4 : 3 - 4   (N K J V)

SIX

FAMILY
Providing a Lifetime of Hugs

Goals

Bound

When does a family begin? With marriage? With the arrival of the first child? It begins whenever committed love defines the goals and boundaries in a place called home. Families are not automatically filled with love and support. People make decisions to live sacrificially for one another. They make choices to live in a way that promotes health and peace. ◆ And true families are not dependent upon times and circumstances. They weather every season together. They determine to finish life's race as a team. Because they are locked together in love, one person's weakness is upheld by others' strength. When one person must endure trials, the others are by his side. When one person has reason to celebrate, she has a ready-made party in the loved ones around her.

◆ Without a family there is no home. And without a home, what are we but orphans, struggling through life under our own power? How wise God was to create the environment and companionship we know as family.

74

nurturing

The kids and I are similar to a valuable piece of farmland with rich soil that would quickly become overgrown with brambles and thorns if it weren't cared for properly. Fortunately my wife is a master gardener. Every day, in many ways, she lovingly cares for me and our family. Primarily because of her skills at nurturing an intimate relationship, we've got a garden that's the envy of all our neighbors.

bright
I've got a family who acts like a flashlight to me. When I'm lost or in the dark, sure enough—I see their light, piercing through the darkness, coming toward me. Then they lead me home to safety. At times they even point their light on a problem area in my life that I've been trying to keep in the dark. I've learned to appreciate that.

Fix these words of mine in your hearts and minds; tie them as symbols on your hands and bind them on your foreheads. Teach them to your children, talking about them when you sit at home and when you walk along the road, when you lie down and when you get up. Write them on the doorframes of your houses and on your gates, so that your days and the days of your children may be many in the land that the Lord swore to give your forefathers, as many as the days that the heavens are above the earth.

DEUTERONOMY 11:18-21

support

My family is like a soft, overstuffed recliner chair, complete with every option and extra the manufacturer has ever made. My family members' words are the warm and soothing heating element, their hugs the massagers that ease the aches and pains of life. With them around I can tip way back but never fall to the ground. After spending time in my chair, I've got the rest and the loving support to keep going.

harmony

I feel like a seed that contains every God-given ingredient needed to grow and be fruitful. Yet I'm dependent on others to provide the water, soil, and sunshine so I can sprout and develop.

*T*o sum up,
let all be
harmonious,
sympathetic,
brotherly,
kindhearted,
and humble
in spirit.

1 PETER 3:8

(NASB)

circus

My friends are like family. We're sort of a happy clown circus, and we do some of the craziest things! We perform so that our people can enjoy life's all-too-rare moments of laughter. But when the performance is over, we can take off our masks and accept each other for who we really are.

PHOTO CONTRIBUTORS

Dean Abramson: 6
Brad Baskin: 1
Timothy R. Botts: 48, 49, 51, 52, 53
James Carroll: 76, 25, 27
CLEO Photography: viii, 2, 12, 14, 19, 20, 35, 44, 62, 67, 81
Luke Golobitsh: 61
Harry Cutting: 28, 32, 37
David Dobbs: 57
Cheryl Ertelt: 36
Chip Henderson: 81
Jean-Claude Lejeune: vi, 30, 60, 72, 80, 83
Jonathan A. Meyers: 2, 22–23, 55
Marilyn Nolt: 29
North American Mission Board, SBC: 5, 10, 11, 15, 30, 32, 36, 39, 41, 46, 47, 56, 58, 68, 69, 70, 71, 72, 78, 80
S W Productions: 2
Wycliffe: vii, 9, 14, 16, 21, 24, 30, 33, 34, 42, 43, 44, 58, 64–65, 74–75, 77, 79.

The goal of Wycliffe Bible Translators USA:

"To assist the church in making disciples of all nations
through Bible translation."

Accomplishing this exciting task requires the prayers of
God's people and the teamwork of people with a wide
variety of skills and occupations.

For information on how you can help, call
1-800-WYCLIFFE (1-800-992-5433), or check out
Wycliffe's Web site at www.wycliffe.org.

**The goal of the North American Mission Board
of the Southern Baptist Convention:**

"Mobilizing for kingdom mission."

God is at work in the world to bring people into a relationship
with him through Jesus Christ. We see a day when every person
in every community in the United States and Canada will have
the opportunity to hear the gospel, respond with faith in Christ,
and participate in a New Testament fellowship of believers.
Therefore, we will work in cooperative partnerships to mobilize
Christians and local churches to reach their communities with
the gospel and establish effective congregations.